DELORES' THESAURUS

A

Aberrant \ab-er-ent\
synonyms: bizarre, strange, odd;
antonyms: common, normal,
usual

Absurd \ab-sur-d\
synonyms: wacky, insane, weird;
antonyms: sane, sensible, smart

Alarming \uh-larm-ing\
synonyms: scary, terrifying,
shocking; **antonyms:** calming,
comforting, relaxing

Aloof \a-loo-f\
synonyms: frosty, standoffish,
unsociable; **antonyms:** friendly,
social, warm

Ambition \am-bish-ion\
synonyms: goal, dream, ideal

Amicable \am-ick-uh-bul\
synonyms: friendly, chummy,
warmhearted; **antonyms:**
hostile, unkind, unfriendly

Archaic \ar-kay-ick\
synonyms: out-of-date, rusty,
dated; **antonyms:** modern,
renewed, operating

Astound \uh-st-ow-nd\
synonyms: amaze, surprise,
stun; **antonyms:** bewilder, daze,
confuse

Astronomical
\as-tro-nom-ick-al\
synonyms: huge, super, gigantic;
antonyms: tiny, miniature, little

Atrocious \uh-tro-sh-es\
synonyms: horrible, frightful,
terrible; **antonyms:** attractive,
pleasant, comforting

Attaché \a-tah-shay\
synonyms: suitcase, bag,
briefcase

Attribute \ah-tri-bute\
synonyms: quality, feature, trait

Audacious \aw-day-sh-uh-s\
synonyms: brazen, wise,
assertive; **antonyms:** meek, shy,
timid

B

Beaming \bee-ming\
synonyms: radiant, glowing,
happy; **antonyms:** flat, stoic,
gloomy

Bellow \bell-oh\
synonyms: holler, screech, cry;
antonyms: mumble, mutter,
whisper

Burgeoning \burr-juh-ning\
synonyms: building up,
increasing, multiplying;
antonyms: decreasing,
dwindling, lessening

Burgle \burr-gull\
synonyms: rob, steal, take

C

Careen \cuh-reen\
synonyms: lurch, hurtle, streak

Composition \comp-o-zish-un\
synonyms: report, discussion,
commentary

Concoct \con-cawk-t\
synonyms: invent, think up,
devise; **antonyms:** copy, mimic,
replicate

Confounded \con-fown-ded\
synonyms: baffled, perplexed,
confused; **antonyms:** unfazed,
untroubled, composed

Creations \cree-ay-shuns\
synonyms: designs, products,
inventions; **antonyms:** copies,
duplicates, replicas

D

Desist \dee-sis-t\
synonyms: stop, halt, quit;
antonyms: continue, proceed,
propel

Dictionary \dic-shun-air-e\
synonyms: lexicon, wordbook,
glossary

E

Eavesdrop \e-vs-drop\
synonyms: listen, spy, snoop

Equatorial \eh-qua-tor-e-al\
synonyms: low, tropical;
antonyms: polar, temperate

Essential \eh-sen-shal\
synonyms: critical, necessary,
required; **antonyms:**
unnecessary, needless,
inessential

Exasperate \ex-as-per-ate\
synonyms: annoy, bother,
infuriate; **antonyms:** delight,
please, assure

Exclusive \ex-cloo-siv\
synonyms: entire, undivided,
focused; **antonyms:** diffuse,
divided, scattered

Excruciating
\ex-crew-she-ate-ing\
synonyms: hard, harsh,
tough; **antonyms:** comfortable,
agreeable, relaxing

Exquisite \ex-quiz-it\
synonyms: fancy, exceptional,
special; **antonyms:** average,
common, inferior

F

Fare \fay-er\
synonyms: chow, food, eats;
antonyms: poison, toxin

Feeble \fee-bul\
synonyms: delicate, weak, frail;
antonyms: healthy, strong,
powerful

Finesse \fuh-ness\
synonyms: cleverness,
efficiency, ingenuity; **antonyms:**

SYNONYMS
ANTONYMS

·DOT·

Flutter \fl-uh-tur\
synonyms: flit, zip, dart;
antonyms: float, hang, hover

Fowl \fa-owl\
synonyms: bird, winged animal,
flying animal

Frantically \fran-tic-a-lee\
synonyms: wildly, haphazardly,
crazily; **antonyms:** calmly,
tamely, composedly

G

Gargantuan \gar-gan-choo-in\
synonyms: huge, gigantic,
massive; **antonyms:** small, mini,
tiny

Gulp \gull-p\
synonyms: swallow, swig, drink

H

Horrified \hor-if-eyed\
synonyms: frightened, afraid,
spooked; **antonyms:** fearless,
brave, courageous

I

Impudence \im-pu-den-s\
synonyms: disrespect, rudeness,
boldness; **antonyms:** humility,
modesty, grace

Indeed \in-deed\
synonyms: certainly, clearly,
definitely

Indubitably \in-doob-it-uh-blee\
synonyms: inarguable, positive,
undeniable; **antonyms:** debated,
inconclusive, uncertain

Infuriate \inf-yur-e-ate\
synonyms: aggravate, irritate,
enrage; **antonyms:** relieve,
appease, comfort

L

Languid \lain-gwid\
synonyms: limp, lazy, sleepy;
antonyms: active, eager,
enthusiastic

M

Milling \mill-ing\
synonyms: wandering, strolling,
traipsing

N

Nefarious \ne-fair-e-us\
synonyms: bad, rotten, wicked;
antonyms: decent, correct,
wholesome

O

Outlandish \out-lan-dish\
synonyms: fantastic, exotic,
strange; **antonyms:** familiar,
unglamorous, plain

P

Patron \pay-tren\
synonyms: consumer, guest,
customer; **antonyms:** seller,
merchant, vendor

Pauper \paw-per\
synonyms: broke, penniless,
destitute; **antonyms:** wealthy,
rich, well-off

Perambulate \per-am-bu-late\
synonyms: navigate, proceed,
travel

Perplexed \per-plex-d\
synonyms: baffled, confused,
stumped; **antonyms:** assured,
enlightened, informed

Persist \per-sis-t\
synonyms: carry on, persevere,
hang on; **antonyms:** quit, give
up, give in

Plague \play-guh\
synonyms: torture, torment,
curse; **antonyms:** assist,
comfort, console

Plea \pl-ee\
synonyms: appeal, desire,
petition

Plight \ply-t\
synonyms: trouble, bind

Potential \po-ten-shall\
synonyms: possible, probable,
viable; **antonyms:** actual,
existent, real

Precisely \pre-sice-lee\
synonyms: exactly, sharp, justly

Prodigious \pro-di-jus\
synonyms: amazing, awesome,
marvelous; **antonyms:**
unimpressive, unremarkable,
boring

Provoke \pro-vo-k\
synonyms: incite, stir, taunt;
antonyms: calm, soothe, subdue

Pursuit \purr-sue-t\
synonyms: hobby, recreation,
amusement

Q

Quip \qu-ip\
synonyms: josh, jest, joke

R

Remarkable \re-mar-kuh-bol\
synonyms: unforgettable,
noteworthy, memorable;
antonyms: average,
unmemorable, forgettable

S

Sprightly \spri-tuh-lee\
synonyms: peppy, animated,
cheerful; **antonyms:** lazy, sleepy,
weary

Stat \st-at\
synonyms: pronto, right away,
instantly; **antonyms:** slowly,
late, tardily

T

Thesaurus \thuh-sore-us\
synonyms: wordfinder,
wordbook, synonym dictionary

V

Valuable \val-u-ah-bul\
synonyms: precious, pricey,
costly; **antonyms:** cheap,
inexpensive, worthless

W

Wail \way-el\
synonyms: groan, moan, sob;
antonyms: cheer, laugh, rejoice

Wharf \war-f\
synonyms: landing, pier, dock

DELORES
THESAURUS

SYNONYMS

ANTONYMS

Written by
Jessica Lee Hutchings
Illustrated by
Hazel Quintanilla

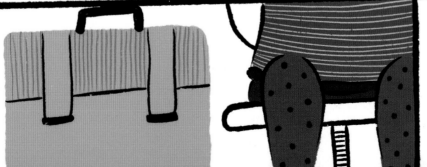

Designed by Flowerpot Press
www.FlowerpotPress.com
DJS-0912-0175
ISBN: 978-1-4867-1463-6
Made in China/Fabriqué en Chine
Copyright © 2018 Flowerpot Press,
a Division of Flowerpot Children's Press,
Inc., Oakville, ON, Canada and Kamalu
LLC, Franklin, TN, U.S.A. All rights

Delores Thesaurus with her pink attaché
put on her coat and her purple beret,
then went out with Dot, her pet Bouvier,
with a plan to collect the big words grown-ups say.

She treated big words like a valuable jewel,
a love she had learned from Ms. Meyers at school.
When she asked her, "Ms. Meyers, do big words suit me?"
Ms. Meyers responded, "INDUBITABLY!"

Ms. Meyers could easily have just answered yes,
but indubitably had so much more finesse.
So Delores had picked up this fine attribute
and made finding big words her exclusive pursuit.

She would go out with Dot exploring the town,
spotting big words and writing them down.
Wherever she looked there were words to be found,
like outlandish and languid, aloof and astound.

With her attaché filled with the words she had seen,
she'd go back to Ms. Meyers to learn what they mean.
"Delores Thesaurus!" Ms. Meyers would say.
"I love the new words that you found yesterday."

She loved learning new ways to say what she meant.
So she kept on collecting everywhere that she went.

She would go to the park and eavesdrop on a parent.
"My child's behavior was atrocious, nefarious, aberrant!"

"Nefarious?!?" she wondered. "That doesn't sound good."
And she made plans to use it the first chance she could.

When she heard a word that had left her confounded,
she listened real closely to be sure how it sounded.
With her favorite green pen she would write the word down,
then continue exploring the rest of the town.

She would go to the market to listen to shoppers.
"These prices are astronomical! They'll make us all paupers!"

She would go to the library to hear college students.
"The hero, while audacious, is plagued with impudence."

She would go to the café to monitor the patrons.
"This fare is exquisite. What remarkable creations!"

Delores told Dot, "Let's perambulate this way.
Off to find more grown-ups and the big words they say!"

Then she walked to the wharf, where she overheard sailors.
"I assure you, Ahab, we are prodigious as whalers!"

She took these great words that she'd heard around town,
listening closely and writing them down,
and placed them all carefully inside her case,
which was now getting full and had run out of space.

She was excited for Ms. Meyers to explain each new word,
until SWOOSH from above something alarming occurred.
A pelican swooped down, grabbed her pink attaché,
gulped it up in its beak, and flew swiftly away.

Delores was horrified and yelled out to say,
"That gargantuan pelican has my words of the day!
STOP! DESIST!" Delores cried out and wailed.
She ran fast, reached high, but her efforts all failed.

Delores ran to the grown-ups all milling around.
She jumped and she shouted. Dot flipped upside down.
But no one stopped to help and no one seemed to listen.
So Delores concocted a more grown-up composition.

"We should use some big words!" she shouted to Dot.
"So they'll stop and they'll help us. It's our only shot!"
She thought back to the new words that they had collected
but couldn't be sure which ones should be selected.

"What words do I remember that I can now use?"
thought Delores as she approached a man reading the news.
"Pardon me, sir, my attaché was languid indeed!"
"Oh, that's nice," he replied and continued to read.

"Drat!" Delores cried. "That word can't be right!"
Then she turned to a woman, hoping she'd see their plight.
"Miss, my attaché was outlandish today!"
"That's too bad," quipped the lady as she went on her way.

Meanwhile...the pelican flew on. It fluttered and soared
with her pink attaché and the words she had scored.

Delores persisted. The mailman was next.
But when she approached him, he just seemed perplexed.
"Sir, can you help? My attaché took an archaic careen."
"I'm sorry, young lady, I don't know what you mean."

"Still not right!" huffed Delores as she searched 'round the crowd.

"Please help! Anyone! Help me!" she bellowed out loud.

"Everything alright, young lady?" a shopkeeper asked.

"No! Exasperate my attaché! I have been excruciatingly tasked!"

The shopkeeper responded, "Hmm...what was that?"
Delores said, "My attaché! It's equatorial, stat!
We must hurry! The feeble fowl burgled my case!"
The shopkeeper was puzzled, but made an amicable face.

"So a bird has your briefcase? Have I got that part right?"
Delores nodded frantically and lit up like a light.
"I wonder," said the shopkeeper as she pointed in the air,
"if perhaps it's that bird that is sitting up there?"

Then the three of them chased the big bird down the pier,
and they called to the pelican, "Hey pelican, come here!"
"It really likes your case," the shopkeeper joked.
"It probably won't drop it unless it's provoked."
So Dot leapt to action, saving the day,
growling and barking for the pink attaché.

The pelican squawked and dropped the attaché,
then flapped its wings hard and flew sprightly away.
Delores ran to the case. She was beaming with pride.
All the words she'd collected were safely inside!

Delores explained all the words she had used
and how everyone responded by looking confused.

The shopkeeper smiled, then made everything clear.
She said to Delores, "Here's the trouble, my dear,
there's a reason your pleas did not go as planned.
When you used your new words they did not understand.
When you said archaic, it really meant out-of-date.
When you said exasperate, it meant infuriate.
When you said careen, it meant to hurtle and streak
and when you used the word feeble, all that meant was weak.
Using big words can sound grown-up indeed.
There's so many fine ways you can say what you need.
And it's clear that in big words you're very well-versed,
but remember it helps to know what they mean first."

Delores giggled, "My words caused such a mess!
I really confused everyone then I guess!"

She held up her case and expressed her unease.
"I wish that I knew how to teach myself these."

"Try this," said the shopkeeper, handing her a worn book.
"I've found this quite useful. You should give it a look."

"A DICTIONARY!" cried Delores. "PRECISELY ESSENTIAL!"
"Thank you so much! This is packed with potential!"

So Delores Thesaurus with her pink attaché
and her burgeoning collection of words grown-ups say
is learning to use them in just the right way
with the lovely worn dictionary she obtained on that day!

Now when Delores Thesaurus finds a new word,
she does not take a chance on sounding absurd.
She looks the word up to know its definition,
and that has filled her with a whole new ambition.

"Using all my new words isn't something I find scary.
In fact, you can call me Delores Dictionary!"

DELORES' DICTIONARY

A

Aberrant \ab-er-ent\
adjective
out of the ordinary

Absurd \ab-sur-d\
adjective
showing a lack of good judgment

Alarming \uh-larm-ing\
adjective
causing fear

Aloof \a-loo-f\
adjective
a lack of friendliness toward others

Ambition \am-bish-ion\
noun
something that one wants to accomplish

Amicable \am-ick-uh-bul\
adjective
showing kindness or sincere interest

Archaic \ar-kay-ick\
adjective
having passed its time of usefulness

Astound \uh-st-ow-nd\
verb
make an impression on someone with something very unexpected

Astronomical
\as-tro-nom-ick-al\
adjective
extremely and unusually big

Atrocious \uh-tro-sh-es
adjective
upsetting or disturbing

Attaché \a-tah-shay\
noun
a small suitcase used for carrying papers

Attribute \ah-tri-bute\
noun
quality that sets someone apart from others

Audacious \aw-day-sh-uh-s\
adjective
displaying boldness, sometimes considered rude

B

Beaming \bee-ming\
verb
displaying good feelings outward

Bellow \bell-oh\
verb
make a long noise or cry

Burgeoning \burr-juh-ning\
verb
growing in amount or number

Burgle \burr-gull\
verb
unlawfully remove valuables

C

Careen \cuh-reen\
verb
make a series of unsteady motions

Composition \comp-o-zish-un\
noun
a short piece of writing expressing a viewpoint

Concoct \con-cawk-t\
verb
create by use of the imagination

Confounded \con-fown-ded\
adjective
faced with uncertainty

Creations \cree-ay-shuns\
noun
something that is created like works of art

D

Desist \dee-sis-t\
verb
bring to an end

Dictionary \dic-shun-air-e\
noun
a reference source filled with words arranged in alphabetical order

E

Eavesdrop \e-vs-drop\
verb
listen in on

Equatorial \eh-qua-tor-e-al\
adjective
near the equator

Essential \eh-sen-shal\
adjective
something you can't do without

Exasperate \ex-as-per-ate\
verb
disturb a person's peace of mind

Exclusive \ex-cloo-siv\
adjective
not divided among other interest areas

Excruciating
\ex-crew-she-ate-ing\
adjective
difficult to endure

Exquisite \ex-quiz-it\
adjective
having appealing qualities

F

Fare \fay-er\
noun
something to eat

Feeble \fee-bul\
adjective
lacking strength

Finesse \fuh-ness\
noun
mental skill

Flutter \fl-uh-tur\
verb
make quick, irregular movements

Fowl \fa-owl\
noun
a bird of any kind

SPANISH WORDS

COOL WORDS

FRENCH WORDS

Frantically \fran-tic-a-lee\
adverb
in a reckless manner

G

Gargantuan \gar-gan-choo-in\
adjective
exceptionally large

Gulp \gull-p\
verb
swallow something at one time

H

Horrified \hor-if-eyed\
adjective
completely filled with fear

I

Impudence \im-pu-den-s\
noun
rude behavior

Indeed \in-deed\
adverb
without question

Indubitably \in-doob-it-uh-blee\
adverb
not able to be proved wrong

Infuriate \inf-yur-e-ate\
verb
make angry

L

Languid \lain-gwid\
adjective
lacking strength

M

Milling \mill-ing\
verb
moving in a circle or wandering

N

Nefarious \ne-fair-e-us\
adjective
morally unacceptable

O

Outlandish \out-lan-dish\
adjective
mysteriously unusual

P

Patron \pay-tren\
noun
someone who buys goods or
uses services provided by an
establishment

Pauper \paw-per\
noun
a very poor person

Perambulate \per-am-bu-late\
verb
make your way through

Perplexed \per-plex-d\
adjective
uncertain

Persist \per-sis-t\
verb
continue even when it is difficult

Plague \play-guh\
verb
cause suffering

Plea \pl-ee\
noun
an important request

Plight \ply-t\
noun
a difficult situation

Potential \po-ten-shall\
adjective
existing as a possibility

Precisely \pre-sice-lee\
adverb
without a slight difference

Prodigious \pro-di-jus\
adjective
causing wonder

Provoke \pro-vo-k\
verb
rouse someone to action

Pursuit \purr-sue-t\
noun
an activity to be engaged in
for fun

Q

Quip \qu-ip\
noun
something said that causes
laughter

R

Remarkable \re-mar-kuh-bol\
adjective
worth mentioning

S

Sprightly \spri-tuh-lee\
adjective
having high-spirited energy

Stat \st-at\
adverb
immediately

T

Thesaurus \thuh-sore-us\
noun
a book of words grouped by
synonyms and related concepts

V

Valuable \val-u-ah-bul\
adjective
marked by a large price

W

Wail \way-el\
verb
cry out in distress

Wharf \war-f\
noun
structure used by boats

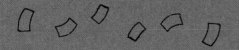